The Hoboken
Chicken
Emergency

Prentice-Hall, Inc., Englewood Cliffs, New Jersey

THE HOBOKEN CHICKEN EMERGENCY

by D. Manus Pinkwater

Printed in the United States of America

Prentice-Hall International, Inc., London
Prentice-Hall of Australia, Pty. Ltd.,
    North Sydney
Prentice-Hall of Canada, Ltd., Toronto
Prentice-Hall of India Private Ltd., New Delhi
Prentice-Hall of Japan, Inc., Tokyo
Prentice-Hall of Southeast Asia Pte. Ltd.,
    Singapore

10 9 8 7 6 5 4 3 2 1

Library of Congress Cataloging in Publication Data

Pinkwater, Manus.
    The Hoboken chicken emergency.

    SUMMARY: Arthur goes to pick up the turkey for
Thanksgiving dinner but comes back with a 260-pound
chicken.
    [1. Chickens—Fiction.   2. Humorous stories]
I. Pinkwater, Manus.   II. Title.
PZ7.P6335Ho   [Fic]   76—41910
ISBN 0—13—392514—5

To Lugo and de Palma,
great men and friends to all chickens.

Books by D. Manus Pinkwater

Bear's Picture

Blue Moose

Fat Elliott and the Gorilla

Lizard Music

Magic Camera

The Terrible Roar

Three Big Hogs

Wingman

Wizard Crystal

The
Hoboken Chicken
Emergency

I

Nobody in Arthur Bobowicz's family really liked turkey. Certainly, the kids didn't like it as much as chicken or duck. They suspected that Momma and Poppa didn't like it very much either. Still, they had a turkey every Thanksgiving, like almost every family in Hoboken. "Thanksgiving is an important American holiday," Poppa would say, "You kids are Americans, and you ought to celebrate important American holidays. On Thanksgiving, you eat turkey. Would you want people to think you were ungrateful?" Poppa came from Poland, and he was very big on holidays, and being an American. There was no arguing with him. They had turkey every year.

Most of the kids in the neighborhood had the same scene at home. Some of them liked turkey, some of them didn't—but they all had it on Thanksgiving. They all had fathers like Arthur Bobowicz's father—they came from Italy, and the Ukraine, and Puerto Rico, and Hong Kong. The kids were all being raised to be Americans, and everyone's father knew that Americans eat turkey on Thanksgiving. Late in November, in the windows of the stores in Hoboken, where ducks had hung, and sausages, and legs of lamb—turkeys appeared. For the rest of the year, anyone who wanted a turkey would have had to go clear out of town. The turkeys appeared in Hoboken at Thanksgiving, no other time.

It was Arthur's job to go and get the family turkey. Poppa had reserved a turkey weeks in advance at Murphy's Meat Market. On Thanksgiving morning, Arthur was supposed to go to the market and bring back the turkey, a big one. The whole family was going to be there—uncles and aunts, and some cousins, Momma and Poppa, and Arthur's little brother and sister. Bringing back the turkey was an important job. Once it came into the house, all the cooking and rushing out for last-minute things from the store, and all the good smells would start. It was a good holiday, and all the kids enjoyed it —but it would have been even better if they had a duck or a chicken.

Something had gone wrong at Murphy's Meat Market. Somehow Poppa's turkey reservation had gotten lost. Every turkey had some family's name on it—none of them had the name Bobowicz. Arthur ran down Garden Street and up the stairs of the apartment house. He told

his mother about the mistake at the meat market. "Maybe you'd better go back and get two chickens and a duck," his mother said. She was almost smiling, "I'll explain it to your father." Arthur was sure she didn't like turkey either—why wouldn't she admit it?

Things had gone even more wrong than Arthur thought. When he got back to Murphy's Meat Market, there wasn't a single chicken in the place—no ducks either. All they had were turkeys, and every one of them was reserved for somebody else. Arthur was bothered by this, but not terribly worried. There are lots of stores and markets in Hoboken—German and Italian butchers, Spanish groceries, supermarkets. You can get almost anything to eat in the world in Hoboken—except a turkey, a chicken, or a duck on Thanksgiving, as Arthur found out. He went to every store in town that might possibly have a bird. He went to a few stores that probably did not have birds—just in case. "This is a fish market! What makes you think we'd have turkeys or chickens, you silly kid?"

"No chickens in a vegetable store, you silly kid!"

"Silly kid! This is an Indian spice store. Curry powder, we've got; mango chutney, we've got; flash-frozen chapatis, we've got—birds we do not have."

Arthur was looking for turkeys, chickens, ducks, geese—he would have taken any kind of bird at all. There wasn't anything of the kind to be found in the whole town. It was getting to be late in the morning, and it was snowing a little. Arthur was getting depressed.

This was the first time he had the job of getting the Thanksgiving bird, and he had messed it up. He had tried everyplace; he had sixteen dollars in his pocket, and he hadn't found one single bird. He walked along River Street. He didn't want to go home and tell his mother the bad news. He felt tired, and the cold was going right through him. He noticed a card stuck in the window of an apartment house door:

Professor Mazzocchi
Inventor of the Chicken System
By appointment

Arthur rang the bell. What did he have to lose? The door-buzzer buzzed, and he pushed it open. He stood at the bottom of the stairs. A voice from above shouted, "You will not get me evicted! My brother owns this building! I am a scientist! If you people don't stop bothering me, I'll let the rooster loose again!"

"Do you have a chicken for sale?" Arthur shouted— he was desperate.

"What? You want to buy a chicken? Come right up!" the voice from above answered. Arthur climbed the stairs. At the head of the stairs was an old man. He was wearing an old bathrobe with dragons embroidered on it. "I have been waiting for years for someone to come to buy a superchicken," the old man said. "The only people who ever come here are neighbors to complain about my chickens. They don't want me to keep them."

"You keep chickens in your apartment?" Arthur asked.

"A farm would be better," Professor Mazzocchi said, "but my brother lets me stay here without paying any rent. Also they are special chickens. I prefer to keep them under lock and key."

"We need one to cook for Thanksgiving," Arthur said.

"A large family?" Professor Mazzocchi asked. "All my cousins are coming," Arthur said.

"And how much money did you bring?" the old man asked, "sixteen dollars? Good. Wait here." The old man went inside the apartment with Arthur's sixteen dollars. When he opened the door, Arthur heard a clucking sound, but not like any clucking he had ever heard —it was deeper, louder. Arthur had a feeling that this wasn't going to work out.

He was right. Professor Mazzocchi came out of the apartment a few minutes later. He was leading a chicken that was taller than he was. "This is the best poultry bargain on earth," he said, "a medium sized superchicken —six cents a pound—here's your two hundred and sixty-six pound chicken, on the hoof. She'll be mighty good eating. Please don't forget to return the leash and collar," and Professor Mazzocchi closed the apartment door.

Arthur stood on the landing with the giant chicken for a while. The chicken looked bored. She shifted from foot to foot, and stared at nothing with her little red eyes. Arthur was trying to understand what had just happened. He was trying to believe there was a two hundred and sixty-six pound chicken standing in the

6

hallway with him. Arthur was feeling numb.

Then Arthur found himself pounding on Professor Mazzocchi's door. "No refunds!" Professor Mazzocchi shouted, without opening the door.

"Don't you have anything smaller?" Arthur shouted.

"No refunds!" Professor Mazzocchi, Inventor of the Chicken System, shouted. Arthur could see that this was all he was going to get from Professor Mazzocchi. He picked up the end of the leash.

"She is a bargain, when you consider the price per pound," Arthur thought. The chicken tamely followed Arthur down the stairs.

Everybody noticed the chicken as Arthur led it home. Most people didn't want to get too close to it. Some people made a sort of moaning noise when they saw the chicken. Arthur and the chicken arrived at the apartment house where the Bobowicz family lived. Arthur led the chicken up the stairs and tied the leash to the bannister. Then he went in to prepare his mother. "That took a long time," she said, "did you get a bird?"

"I got a chicken," Arthur said.

"Well, where is it?" his mother asked.

"I left it in the hall," Arthur said, "It only cost six cents a pound."

"That's very cheap," his mother said, "Are you sure there's nothing wrong with it? Maybe it isn't fresh."

"It's fresh," Arthur said, "It's alive."

"You brought home a live chicken?" his mother was getting excited.

"It was the only one I could find," Arthur started to cry, "I went to all the stores, and nobody had any turkeys or chickens or ducks, and finally I bought this chicken from an old man who raises them in his apartment."

Arthur's mother was headed for the door, "Momma, it's a very big chicken!" Arthur shouted. She opened the door. The chicken was standing there, shifting from foot to foot, blinking.

"CLUCK," it said. Arthur's mother closed the door, and just stood staring at it. She didn't say anything for a long time.

Finally she said, "There's a two-hundred pound chicken in the hall," she was talking to the door.

"Two-hundred and sixty-six pounds," Arthur said; he was still sobbing.

"Two hundred and sixty-six pounds of live chicken," his mother said, "It's wearing a dog collar."

"I'm supposed to return that," Arthur said. Arthur's mother opened the door and peeked out. Then she closed the door again. She looked at Arthur. She opened the door and looked at the chicken.

"She seems friendly, in a dumb way," she said.

"I thought we could call her Henrietta," Arthur said. "You were supposed to bring home an ordinary chicken to eat," Arthur's mother said, "Not a two hundred and sixty-six pound chicken to keep as a pet."

"It was the only one I could find," Arthur said.

Arthur's little brother and sister had been watching all this from behind the kitchen door. "Please let us

8

keep her," they shouted, "we'll help Arthur feed her, and walk her, and take care of her."

"She walks on the leash very nicely," Arthur said, "I can train her, and she can cluck if burglars ever come. She's a good chicken, PLEASE!"

"Put her in the kitchen, and we'll discuss it when your father comes home," Arthur's mother said.

That night the family had meatloaf, and mashed potatoes, and vegetables for Thanksgiving dinner. Everybody thought it was a good meal. Henrietta especially liked the mashed potatoes, although Poppa warned everybody not to feed her from the table. "I don't want this chicken to get into the habit of begging," he said, "and the first time the children forget to feed or walk her—out she goes."

Poppa had decided to let Arthur keep Henrietta. "Every boy should have a chicken," he said.

II

Arthur got up early the day after Thanksgiving, to take Henrietta for a walk. Before going out, Arthur made a cup of instant cocoa for himself, and gave Henrietta the leftover mashed potatoes. It was just getting to be daylight when he led Henrietta out into the street. She was blinking. Arthur thought that Henrietta might enjoy a walk by the river. They started walking East on Fourth Street. There wasn't a single person in the street —it was too early. An empty bus was headed down Washington Street. The driver saw Henrietta, and ran into a garbage can. It was one of those wire ones. It got a little bent, but the bus wasn't damaged. There was a cold wind ruffling Henrietta's feathers. Arthur zipped up his jacket.

Near the river there was an iron fence that ran all

along River Street. Beyond it were the docks, where all the big ships came in. There was a place in the fence big enough for a kid to squeeze through. Arthur had squeezed through it lots of times, early in the morning. He liked to walk around and look at the ships before the dockers came and got busy loading and unloading. He forgot about getting Henrietta through the hole in the fence. She was much too big. Arthur tried to get her to jump over the fence—he wasn't sure whether she could do it or not—but he couldn't get the idea across. He whistled, and clapped his hands, and tugged on Henrietta's leash—but she just blinked at him. Arthur was starting to get the idea that chickens aren't very smart. The night before, while Henrietta was sleeping next to his bed, Arthur had made plans to teach her a lot of tricks. Now it didn't seem very likely that he was going to have an easy time of teaching her anything.

Once Arthur was satisfied that he couldn't get Henrietta to jump the fence onto the docks, he led her up River Street to the park. There was some playground equipment there—swings, slides, a jungle-gym. One of the reasons Arthur liked to get up extra-early was that he could fool around with the playground stuff without any of his friends seeing him. It was really stuff for little kids—Arthur's brother and sister played on it. Kids Arthur's age didn't fool around with slides and that sort of thing.

Arthur sat on a swing. He let Henrietta loose, and she pecked at the playground gravel. Arthur twisted the swing around and around, until the chains were twisted in a long spiral—then he let it unwind, spinning him slowly, while he dragged his toe in the gravel. His toe pushed gravel in front of it, and made a groove with a ridge of gravel on either side—a circle under the swing.

Henrietta continued to peck at the ground. She was clucking to herself. She seemed content. "Henrietta!" Arthur called. She didn't even look up. He clapped his hands, "Henrietta! Come here!" Henrietta blinked at him. Arthur jumped off the swing and started walking away, "O.K., just stay here by yourself!" he said. Henrietta galloped after him, crashed into him, and, after they had both gotten their balance, followed Arthur around the playground clucking. She wasn't all that stupid—just slow—and clumsy. "Heel, Henrietta, heel, girl," Arthur said. Every now and then Arthur would run a few steps, and Henrietta would scurry to catch up with him. She was doing pretty well for a chicken who had never been trained before. Arthur was having fun. Every now and then he would pat Henrietta on the back, and scratch her neck feathers. She liked that. She stretched her neck, and made a sort of cooing noise.

There was a day off from school—Thanksgiving vacation, and Arthur knew that some kids would be along in an hour or so. He had Henrietta pretty well trained to follow him. That would go over pretty well—but if he could teach her one or two more tricks, then he could really impress people. He taught her to swing on the swings. It was easy. First Arthur jumped up on the swing,

and stood on the seat. Then he got off and did it again —to show Henrietta what he wanted. Then Arthur got Henrietta following him pretty fast, and jumped over the seat of the swing. She jumped over it too. They did that a couple of times. Next, Arthur jumped over the seat, spun around, put his hands out in front of him and shouted, "Stay!" Henrietta remained perched on the swing, waving her wings in the air for balance. "Goood, chicken," Arthur said. She caught on pretty fast. After a few tries, Henrietta would jump up on the swing when Arthur said "Hup!" Then Arthur would get behind her, and swing her—not too fast. Henrietta seemed to be enjoying the whole procedure.

Arthur wasn't through yet. He needed something for a big finish. He decided to try the slide. It was a little more complicated than the swing, but Arthur thought Henrietta might be able to do it—she was certainly enthusiastic—Arthur could tell from her expression. The hard part was the ladder. Arthur was ready to give up a couple of times. Henrietta just couldn't get the idea at first. She would stand on the first rung, waving her wings, the way she had on the swing. After a while she would jump off, backwards. Arthur tried getting her to follow him up. He tried calling her from the top of the ladder. Nothing worked. Finally, he just got under her and pushed with all his might—she hopped up one step. "Gooood chicken," Arthur said. Henrietta jumped off backwards and nearly landed on him. Still, she had hopped up one step. She could do it. The rest was just practice. When Henrietta finally got to the top, she discovered that she liked sliding down. After being led around to the ladder by Arthur the first couple of times, she learned to run around after each slide, climb the ladder, and slide down again. She seemed to never get tired of it, and would keep sliding until Arthur shouted, "Henrietta, heel!" She looked good doing it. Arthur had a great finish for his trained chicken act. Arthur had thought ahead enough to fill his jacket pockets with oatmeal cookies. When he thought that Henrietta had enough training for one day, he gave her some cookies as a reward. He scratched her head, and stroked her neck, "Goood chicken!" Arthur waited for some kids to turn up.

Arthur sat on a swing tossing broken bits of oatmeal cookie to Henrietta. She was learning to catch them in mid-air—a small trick, but it gave Arthur something to do for an encore. People were leaving their houses to go to work. There was traffic outside the little park. No one bothered to look over and see a boy in a swing feeding cookies to a two-hundred-and sixty-six pound chicken. Arthur felt good. He was really getting to like Henrietta a lot, he didn't have to go to school, and he was planning to amaze his friends. His friends would just be sitting down to breakfast now. Momma and Poppa would be noticing that he and Henrietta were gone. They wouldn't be worried; Arthur often sneaked out early. Momma would give him a lecture about eating a well-balanced breakfast, but it wouldn't be too serious. Arthur didn't sneak out early every day. And today was special anyway —it was his first day with Henrietta, and the day after Thanksgiving.

A door opened to a house across the street from the park, and something mostly black, and big and fast came out, bounded across the street, over the fence and into the park. It was Bozo. Arthur knew most of the dogs in Hoboken. People in Hoboken often let their dogs loose in the morning, and don't expect them back until suppertime. The dogs wander around, meet other dogs, knock over garbage cans, get into trouble, and wander home around six-o-clock. Bozo was a big German Shepherd. Arthur knew him. He wasn't a bad dog, but he was sort of a bully. He liked to bark at people, and try to scare them, and he pushed other dogs around. Bozo's first stop every morning was the park. He thought it was his park, and he ran all around it every morning, barking at people he met, and chasing out any dogs who had gotten there before him. He ran straight at Arthur and Henrietta, but he wasn't really looking at them. They were just in the path of his usual first run across the playground. Bozo and Henrietta saw each other at the same time. Both of them made a loud noise. Henrietta said, "Awwk!" and jumped ten or fifteen feet straight up in the air.

Bozo said, "Eeeep!" and skidded to a stop. Arthur was impressed with the jump Henrietta had made. That fence was going to be no problem at all, next time. The dog and the chicken were staring at each other—

frozen. All of Bozo's fur was standing straight up, like a cartoon. Henrietta's feathers were all fluffed up. They stood that way, it seemed like, a long time. Then they both took off. They went in opposite directions. Bozo went South. Henrietta went North. Arthur was on his feet, running after her in less than a second, but she was over the fence, out of the park, and two blocks up Hudson Street so fast that Arthur could hardly believe it. Even though he was running hard, he felt as though he were standing still as the big chicken got smaller and smaller, running up the street, and finally disappeared.

III

"Bozo, you dumb dog! You scared my chicken!" Arthur was running as fast as he could up Hudson Street. Bozo watched him through the playground fence. His tongue was lolling out, his tail was wagging. He was proud of himself, the idiot. He watched as Arthur ran up the street for a few blocks, and then trotted off to find more adventures.

Arthur came to the spot where Henrietta had seemed to disappear. He slowed down to a walk and began looking everywhere a two hundred and sixty-six pound chicken could possibly hide. "Henrietta! Here girl! Good chicken!" Arthur called. There was no sign of her. Arthur was just a couple of blocks from a big cross street. There were people and cars, and a bunch of men fixing the street. If Henrietta had passed that corner somebody would certainly have noticed. Arthur asked everyone if they had seen a chicken. Nobody had. Henrietta hadn't come that way. Arthur retraced his steps, back down Hudson Street to the place he had lost sight of his chicken. "Henrietta!" No answer. He looked up and down the side streets, in the alley, in basement doors, and behind shrubbery. No chicken. Arthur was getting confused. A chicken that big couldn't just vanish into thin air. Arthur went over the ground again. This time he looked into apartment house doorways and hallways. Maybe Henrietta was hiding inside. No luck. What if somebody had grabbed her—was going to cook her? Arthur suddenly had the panicky thought of an old Italian lady making soup. "HENRIETTA!" Arthur was starting to cry. Where could she be?

CLUCK——where had that come from? Arthur wondered if he was starting to hear things. CLUCK, he heard it again. "Henrietta! Henrietta!" CLUCK. CLUCK. The sound was coming from overhead.

Arthur looked up. Henrietta was in a tree. She was about three stories above the sidewalk. "Henrietta! Come down!" Arthur said.

"CLUCK," Henrietta said. She looked worried. It was pretty clear to Arthur that she was stuck, like a cat. She could climb, or jump, or fly up—but she couldn't get down.

"Henrietta, fly down," Arthur called to her, but he knew it was no use—she was stuck for sure. Arthur thought he would go and get the fire department. They

got cats out of trees, and this was the same thing, more or less. A woman opened the curtains of a window three floors up—directly opposite the tree in which Henrietta was sitting. She looked out.

"CLUCK," Henrietta said. Arthur couldn't hear, but he could see the woman's open mouth and staring eyes. It lasted a long time. Then the woman closed the curtains, and Arthur went to get the fire department. He didn't have to bother. The lady who screamed had called the fire department, the police department, the mayor's office, and her sister in Jersey City.

Arthur had not gone half-a-block when he heard the sirens. In another minute the red fire trucks were screeching around the corner. "Get off the street, kid!" the firemen shouted, "There's a polar bear loose in a tree!"

"It isn't a polar bear!" Arthur shouted back, "it's a giant chicken, and she belongs to me!" The fire trucks and police cars had come from both ends of the street. The sirens were winding down, and policemen and firemen were slamming doors, and getting portable loudspeakers, hoses and coils of rope ready. People were looking out of windows, and gathering in little groups in front of their apartment house doors.

"Keep back!" a policeman shouted over a loudspeaker, "The polar bear may be dangerous."

"It isn't a polar bear!" Arthur shouted, "It's a chicken,

and she belongs to me!" The policemen and firemen had spotted Henrietta, and were spreading out under the tree.

"Keep back! Keep back!" the policeman kept repeating over the loudspeaker. Other policemen and firemen were talking over the radio—asking headquarters how they were supposed to deal with polar bears in trees.

"It isn't as though the polar bear were on fire." Arthur heard one fireman say into a microphone. Over the radio speaker in a police car, Arthur heard a voice.

"Has there been a complaint that the polar bear is breaking any laws?"

"It isn't a polar bear! It's a chicken, and she's mine!" Arthur shouted, and grabbed the biggest policeman around by the sleeve.

The big policeman spoke into the microphone, "Chief, there's a kid here—says it isn't a polar bear—says it's a chicken, and it belongs to him."

"CLUCK," Henrietta said.

"It clucks," said the big policeman into the microphone.

It took a long time to convince the firemen and policemen that Henrietta was a chicken and not a polar bear. The clucking finally convinced most of them, although there were some arguments among them about what kind of a noise polar bears *do* make. After a while, the firemen put a long ladder up against the tree. Arthur shouted, "Hup!" and Henrietta hopped onto the top rung of the ladder. "Hup!" Arthur shouted again, and she jumped down to the next rung. "Hup! Hup! Hup! Hup!" and Henrietta hopped down the ladder one rung at a time. There was a pretty big crowd by this time, and a man from the newspaper was taking pictures. There were a lot of kids Arthur knew in the crowd. He wished there were a slide nearby. When Henrietta hopped off the last rung, the crowd applauded. Arthur thanked the fire department, told Henrietta, "Heel!" and started for home.

IV

It wasn't Henrietta's fault that dumb Bozo had scared her. It wasn't her fault that she didn' know how to get down from a tree. And leaning on the bannister in the hallway and breaking it really wasn't her fault—it had been loose for years. Arthur's father could have sued the landlord, if she had gotten hurt. Another thing which was not Henrietta's fault was eating the goldfish. She didn't know any better. Arthur had kept his part of the bargain. He had taken Henrietta for walks. He had fed her. Now Poppa had told Arthur to take the chicken back where he had gotten her. It wasn't fair. The picture in the newspaper, of which Arthur was very proud, seemed to have the opposite effect on Poppa.

Poppa was hard to argue with, once he made up his mind. Arthur had to take Henrietta back, that was all there was to it. Poppa said that an apartment was no place to keep a grown chicken—especially one that weighed two hundred and sixty-six pounds.

Arthur rang the bell, and went up the stairs to Professor Mazzocchi's apartment. He was leading Henrietta. "So, it's you," Professor Mazzocchi said, "I told you no refunds, didn't I?"

"I didn't come for a refund," Arthur said. "My father says I can't keep Henrietta. He says I have to give her back. He says you don't have to give back the money. I'm just not supposed to come home until I've gotten rid of her." Arthur was almost crying.

"So, you didn't want to eat her," Professor Mazzocchi said, "I can understand that. Number seventy-three is a very pleasant bird. I never eat chicken myself. In fact I never eat meat, fish, or fowl. Nothing but birdseed and water do I eat, for the past sixty years and more."

"Will you take Henrietta back?" Arthur asked. His nose was running, and he was beginning to sob.

"Yes, my boy. I'll take her back. But you are so sad to think of leaving your nice chicken. Why don't you come in? Maybe I can find some other pet to take her place?"

"I don't want another pet," Arthur said, "I want them to let me keep Henrietta." He was crying for sure now.

"Come in and have a look around anyway," Professor Mazzocchi said, "Maybe you'll see something interesting." The professor opened the door to his apartment, and led Arthur and Henrietta inside. Arthur had never seen anything like Professor Mazzocchi's apartment.

26

There were a lot of big rooms, all of them full of cages, tanks, crates and baskets. So many animals were clucking, and screeching, and howling, and chattering that Arthur couldn't tell one sound from another. It was just one big continuous noise. There were quite a lot of chickens, some bigger than Henrietta. Arthur didn't think any of them were as pretty. There were glass tanks with red-and-blue lizards, cages with birds of every color, and big fish tanks.

"Here's something I am proud of," Professor Mazzocchi said. He pointed to a very large fish tank. Swimming in it were a number of goldfish—large ones—and they were perfectly rectangular. They looked like golden bricks, with tails and fins.

"What are those?" Arthur asked.

"Ah! You're interested in my rectangular goldfish?" Professor Mazzocchi seemed proud, "I'll give you a couple to take the place of your chicken—but I must warn you—they lose their corners after a couple of years."

"I've never seen anything like them," Arthur said, "Where do they come from?"

"Where? Here!" Professor Mazzocchi said, "I raise them myself. If you promise not to tell anyone, I'll explain how it is done."

Arthur promised.

"Did you know that a goldfish will grow according to the size of the tank he is kept in?" Professor Mazzocchi asked. Arthur had not known that. "Oh yes! The little baby goldfish you buy in the dime store, if kept in a bathtub, will grow very large indeed. Of course, it takes time, but it will grow. If you had a big lake to keep it in, and nothing unpleasant happened to it, that little baby goldfish might get to be five feet long in ten or fifteen years. However, if you keep the little baby goldfish in a little baby fishbowl, it will remain a little baby goldfish all its life."

Arthur was fascinated. He made a mental note to keep some goldfish in the bathtub sometime, and see how big they'd get. "But how do you get squared-off goldfish?" he asked.

"Of course! My secret! I do this: I put the little baby goldfish in a medium sized tank. All around the tank I put beautiful oil paintings of the bottom of a lake. The little baby goldfish is very stupid. He doesn't know they are only photographs. Also, when he bumps into the glass walls of his tank, he can't understand that it is glass— so he forgets about it. Fish do not like to think about things they can't understand. So! Thinking the tank is as big as a lake, the goldfish begins to grow. He gets so big that his sides are touching the walls of the tank. Soon he grows to fill the corners. To make the top of the fish flat, I turn him over every so often. Presto! A square fish. The only thing I have to watch out for, is that the fish will displace all the water in his tank, and suffocate. When the fish is nice and square, I put him in a nice big tank, with other nice fishes, and he is very happy."

"But why do you want them to be square?" Arthur asked.

"Why? Why? Because they are easy to stack when they are that shape, you silly boy!" Professor Mazzocchi shouted. "With goldfish it doesn't matter, I admit, but think—if sardines, tunafish, herring were rectangular—how easy it would be to transport them. Just freeze them, and stack them in a boxcar—no wasted space."

The professor offered Arthur a pair of his rectangular goldfish. He offered him a red-and-blue lizard. He said he was working toward a red-white-and-blue one. All he had been able to breed so far were red-and-blue, red-and-white, and white-and-blue. Arthur was interested in the square goldfish, and the brightly colored lizards, but he didn't want to take any of the animals that Professor Mazzocchi offered him. He felt it would be disloyal to Henrietta. Besides, you can love a two-hundred and sixty-six pound chicken. How can you love a square goldfish? Arthur even turned down a special experiment of Professor Mazzocchi's—a bat crossed with a mushroom.

Somehow, being around the professor's apartment, which would have interested Arthur ordinarily, just made him feel sad. The professor was being very nice, and trying to make up for his having to give up Henrietta, but it didn't help at all. Finally Arthur said good-bye to the professor, hugged Henrietta, and went out into the cold street.

V

Arthur knew he'd always be miserable without Henrietta. He knew he could never really forgive his father for not giving her a second chance. In the short time that Henrietta had been with him, Arthur had gotten used to her. When he went to bed that night, it seemed wrong to him that she was not sleeping on the rug next to his bed. He dreamed of chickens—big ones. Arthur was a ringmaster, in his dream. He had a beautiful red coat with gold braid and buttons, and there were maybe fifteen chickens performing tricks. Arthur had a whip. He would snap the whip, and shout, "Hup!" and the chickens would do somersaults, hop onto one another's shoulders, and do headstands. There was a roll of drums, and Arthur shouted, "Hup! Hup! Hup! Hup!" and the chickens began to form a chicken-pyramid. Five chickens stood in a row; then four chickens hopped onto their shoulders; then three chickens; then two; and finally one chicken on top, with an American flag in her beak. It was beautiful—all fifteen chickens making a pyramid more than thirty feet high, waving their wings, and clucking—the flag on top. SNAP SNAP SNAP went the whip, and then, on a huge black horse, Henrietta appeared. She was standing on the horse, on one foot. The horse galloped around and around the pyramid of chickens. Henrietta waved to the crowd. The crowd was going wild. They were cheering. They were screaming, screaming, screaming. They were screaming hysterically.

Arthur was waking up. He could still hear the screaming of the crowd. It didn't sound as much like a crowd now, as it sounded like Mrs. Gluckstern downstairs. It sounded to Arthur as though Mrs. Gluckstern had her head stuck outside the window, and was screaming all sorts of things, like, "HELP!" and "POLICE!" Arthur opened his own window, and poked his head out just in time to see a huge white form scurry down the fire escape that ran past his bedroom window, and Mrs. Gluckstern's. The white thing disappeared into the shadows. Windows opened. Lights were turned on. Mrs. Gluckstern continued to scream, "It was looking right through the venetian blinds! A monster! A gorilla! All white, with red eyes! It was a gorilla as big as a horse!"

The telephone rang. Arthur could hear his father

talking. "No, it wasn't our chicken," Poppa said, "My son got rid of the chicken this afternoon. Maybe it was a burglar in a white overcoat. Just a coincidence." Poppa hung up. Arthur could hear him walking toward Arthur's bedroom. "You did get rid of the chicken, didn't you son?" Poppa asked.

"Yes, Poppa," Arthur said.

The family went back to bed. Arthur had a hard time falling asleep. Had it been a burglar? Maybe Henrietta had gotten loose. She could be looking for him. If she were loose in Hoboken at night, she would probably get scared. Who would feed her? Arthur made up his mind to go to Professor Mazzocchi's early in the morning, just to check up on things, and say hello to Henrietta.

Arthur arrived outside Professor Mazzocchi's apartment house just in time to see the professor locking the doors of a big green truck. AUGIE'S TRUCK RENTAL, it said on the side. From the muffled clucking and screeching, Arthur could tell that all the professor's experiments were inside. "Professor Mazzocchi!" Arthur shouted, "Are you going away?"

"Just for a little while, my boy," Professor Mazzocchi said, "All of a sudden, I feel like visiting my sister in Pennsylvania. I'll be back . . . after a while." The professor was hurrying around, checking the tires.

"Professor, did Henrietta get loose?" Arthur asked.

"*Who told you that?*" the professor looked frightened, "Did someone tell you that number seventy-three was loose?"

"I think I saw her," Arthur said, "I'm worried about her."

"*You're* worried! *You're* worried!" Professor Mazzocchi was getting very excited, "I'm worried! Do you know what happens to people when one of my experiments gets loose? They go crazy! One time they burned down my house! Burned it down! It was a beautiful old castle, and they burned it right to the ground!" Professor Mazzocchi ran around the truck again, making sure that all the doors were locked tight.

"But Professor Mazzocchi," Arthur said, "Henrietta is wandering around the streets of Hoboken, all alone. She must be frightened, and cold, and hungry. Don't you care what happens to her?"

"Of course I care," Professor Mazzocchi said, "but when you've been a mad scientist as long as I have, you learn that some things are more important than others. Most important, right now, is for me to get out of town with all my experiments. If the news gets around that I am responsible for a very large chicken loose in the streets, people will start acting crazy. You and I know that number seventy-three is a very gentle chicken, but people are sometimes afraid of things they've never seen before. When they are afraid, they do foolish things, like burning down other people's castles."

"But what about Henrietta?" Arthur said, "Who's going to take care of her?"

"Look," the professor said, "don't show this to anybody. I'm going to give you my sister's address. If you have any trouble, send me a postcard. I'll help you if I can." The professor wrote something down on a card.

It said: Professor Fritz Mazzocchi
c/o Cosima Mazzocchi
Mooseport, Pa.

Professor Mazzocchi started the engine, and the big green truck rumbled away.

VI

It was Saturday. School would start on Monday. Thanksgiving recess, which had begun on Thursday, would be over. Arthur had less than two days to devote to finding Henrietta. Once he found her, he wasn't sure what he would do. The first thing was to find her. It was cold, and the sky was grey and heavy-looking. It was sure to rain or snow. Arthur thought about Henrietta, huddled in some tree, lost and hungry. It had been Henrietta on the fire escape the night before. She had found the apartment house in which Arthur lived, and even found the fire escape which led to his bedroom window. But Mrs. Gluckstern's screaming had frightened her away. Arthur was worried that she wouldn't be able to find his house again.

Also there was talk in the neighborhood. Some people

still believed it was a polar bear. Some people knew it was a chicken. Some people, like Mrs. Gluckstern, thought it was a white gorilla. Arthur thought about what Professor Mazzocchi had said. He hoped nobody would do anything to hurt Henrietta. He had to find her first—that was all there was to it.

Arthur was careful to check trees and telephone poles, as well as alleys, parks, doorways, and parked cars. He also asked people if they had seen a big chicken. Some of the people had seen the picture of Henrietta in the newspaper. Some people didn't know what Arthur was talking about. Some people warned him to get off the street, because there was a wild gorilla loose. None of the people Arthur asked had seen a chicken. Arthur walked up and down almost every street in town. There was no sign of Henrietta. He went home for lunch.

Poppa had already finished his lunch, and was reading the newspaper. "There are a lot of odd articles in the paper," Poppa said. "Several people have reported seeing a white gorilla in the street. There are also some reports that a polar bear broke into a greengrocer's and ate six bushels of raw potatoes. I think it would be a good idea if nobody in this family said anything about Arthur's chicken. Just let things settle down by themselves."

Arthur ate his tomato soup and veal-loaf on pumpernickel sandwich, and didn't say anything. He was trying to figure out where Henrietta could be hiding. "Maybe we should keep the children inside," Arthur's mother said, "just in case there is a gorilla."

"I don't think there's a gorilla," Poppa said, "but maybe we should keep the children inside just the same."

"I have to go out," Arthur said.

"You've been out all morning," Momma said, "Don't you have some homework to do?"

Arthur saw that he was going to have to sneak out. He didn't like to do that, but this was an emergency. After lunch on Saturday, Poppa always took a nap, and Momma would be busy in the kitchen. Arthur could sneak out of the house easily, if his little brother and sister didn't tell on him. He would have to bribe them with comic books.

Arthur had remembered one place to look for Henrietta that he had not thought of before. Rooftops! If Henrietta could climb fire escapes and ladders, it would be easy for her to get onto a roof. She could hide there all day. Arthur had thought of a way to get a look at all the roofs in Hoboken at once. There was a brand-new apartment building in town. It was so new, it wasn't even finished yet, and it was twenty-five stories tall. It was the only tall building in Hoboken—twenty stories higher than all the other buildings. Arthur had gone with his mother to look at the model apartment, which was an apartment all fixed up as though people lived in it. People could go and look at the model apartment, to see if they wanted to live in the new building. Arthur's mother had no intention of living in the new building —she was afraid of heights. She just wanted to see how the model apartment was decorated. The model apartment was on the nineteenth floor. You could see the whole town from the windows.

Arthur got on the elevator. There was nobody around. He pushed the button which was marked "19" and the elevator went up. His stomach felt funny. When the door opened on the nineteenth floor, Arthur stepped out into the hallway. It was painted pink. It still smelled of paint. The floor of the elevator was covered with plaster dust, and lids from the paper cups that the workmen had their coffee in. Arthur walked to the end of the hall, to the door of the model apartment. He was in luck—it wasn't locked.

It was a very fancy apartment, with all sorts of furniture upholstered in gold velvet, with lots of fancy drapes on the windows. The light fixtures had little crystal things hanging from them, and the carpet was very soft, and almost white. Arthur's mother said it was in bad taste. He went to the window. There was Hoboken, spread out below him. He could see almost the whole town. Arthur looked over the rooftops. They were black, and shiny with the rain that had started to fall. Some of them had pigeon coops on them. There were chimneys, and television antennas. Looking out over the town was so interesting, that Arthur almost forgot to look for Henrietta. Then he saw her. A fluttering of white behind a chimney. That's where she was hiding. Arthur had guessed right. He raced to the elevator. It seemed terribly slow going down. "I should have used the stairs," he thought. When he reached the street, he started running.

"The fourth house from the corner on the East side of Garden Street, near Sixth," he thought. When he got there he realized it was his own house. Of course! Henrietta had sneaked back up the fire escape when everyone had gone back to sleep. Arthur thundered up the stairs, up the little extra flight of stairs, through the little door, and onto the roof. "HENRIETTA!" A wet sheet, that someone had forgotten to take in, was flapping on the clothesline. That was what he had seen from the window of the model apartment.

Arthur sat down with his back against the chimney. The wet roof soaked through the seat of his trousers. He could feel the warmth of the chimney through his jacket. She was still lost. He looked up at the big apartment building. He counted the floors up to the model apartment, where he had been a few minutes ago, where he thought he had seen Henrietta. Seventeen, eighteen, nineteen; Arthur could just make out the triple row of blue velvet curtains. The rain was falling in his face.

On the unfinished twentieth floor, Arthur saw something move. It was white. Arthur squinted. He didn't want to get fooled again. Something big and white was filling up the whole window. Then it was gone. Then it appeared at the next window. Then it moved again, and appeared at another window. It had to be Henrietta. It had to be.

Arthur started down the stairs. "Arthur! Inside!" it was Poppa. "You were supposed to stay inside, and here you are running up and down the stairs, soaking wet!"

42

Poppa said, "Now you'll stay inside, and I mean stay!" Poppa was serious. There was no point in explaining to him. He had told Arthur to get rid of Henrietta, so he was not about to allow him to go after her; second, every kid in town had been told nine million times to stay away from the new high-rise building, from the first day they started building it. Of course, every kid in town had played there, but it was not something you mentioned to your parents. Arthur was marched into the apartment, and ordered into a hot bath.

He would have no chance to go and rescue Henrietta, or even bring her a few oatmeal cookies until late Sunday afternoon. The family was going to visit Aunt Ruth and Arthur's cousins, one more hateful than the next, in Rutherford, early in the morning. Henrietta was on her own for the next twenty-four hours.

VII

Sunday was a misery as Arthur expected it would be. The day with the cousins droned on. It seemed to Arthur that his parents would never go home. Arthur was afraid the big apartment building would be locked by the time he got there. What if Henrietta was locked in overnight? She had been in the big building for two days. What could she find to eat in the empty building? What if the workmen discovered her Monday morning? Arthur thought about pretending to be sick, to get the family started home, but that would only have the effect of getting put in bed, and watched closely, once they got there. He would have to wait until the grown-ups got tired of each other.

Poppa finally had enough. He got his family together and hustled them into the car. It was very late, almost dark. Arthur was in despair. The building was sure to be locked up. Poppa turned on the car radio. . . . AND THOSE ARE THE FOOTBALL SCORES . . . the voice on the radio said. . . . AND NOW, A BIZARRE NEWS STORY FROM HOBOKEN, NEW JERSEY. . . . Arthur and his family stirred and listened. . . . MANY RELIABLE WITNESSES HAVE REPORTED SIGHTINGS OF A GIANT CHICKEN, OR CHICKENS. . . . LAST NIGHT, MORE THAN FIFTY PEOPLE REPORTED CHICKEN SIGHTINGS TO THE POLICE, THE F.B.I., AND THE WHITE HOUSE. . . . THE CHICKENS, WHICH STAND ABOUT FIFTEEN FEET HIGH, AND ARE ESTIMATED TO WEIGH ABOUT ONE THOUSAND POUNDS, ARE SEEN WALKING OR RUNNING THROUGH THE STREETS. . . . THERE HAVE BEEN NO REPORTS OF INJURIES, OR ATTACKS ON PERSONS. . . . THIS RADIO STATION WILL KEEP YOU POSTED ON THE CHICKEN CRISIS IN HOBOKEN.

"Could that be Arthur's chicken?" Momma asked.

"No," Poppa said, "Arthur's chicken was only about two hundred and fifty pounds."

"Two sixty-six," Arthur said.

Arthur remembered how confused people had gotten over whether Henrietta was a polar bear, a gorilla, or a chicken. As far as Arthur knew, Henrietta, or number seventy-three as the professor called her, was the only chicken to escape. It was amazing to Arthur how inac-

curate people could be about an ordinary six-foot tall, two hundred and sixty-six pound chicken. He was sure it was Henrietta they had seen. There weren't any one thousand pound chickens running around Hoboken. It was just Henrietta. That meant she had gotten out of the big apartment building. She was loose in the streets again.

Arthur managed to get out of the house, and spend a couple of hours looking for Henrietta. He didn't have any luck. The next morning, Arthur snuck out early, and looked for Henrietta before he went to school. Again, he didn't find her.

When Arthur arrived at school, the kids gathered outside were talking about the giant chickens. Some said there was one; and some said there were a lot of them. Some of the kids thought they came from a flying saucer. A couple of kids claimed to have seen giant chickens, which interested Arthur, until he heard them say that the chickens were two stories high, and had paralyzer rays. Then he knew they were making it up.

The bell rang, and the kids went inside. Miss Gooseberg handed out programmed reading materials—little cardboard-bound books with pieces of stories in them. Arthur wished they'd get to read a whole story once in a while. It was an ordinary day in school, schoolwork got done, Miss Gooseberg had trouble with the usual kids, the clock ticked. Then there was a scream! It came from somewhere in the building. Everybody jumped. Some kids began to cry immediately. Miss Gooseberg jumped up and ran to the door. There were more screams. They seemed closer. Miss Gooseberg went out into the hall. Then she screamed. Miss Gooseberg staggered back into the room, holding onto the blackboard. She went to her desk, fell into her chair, and put her head on her arms and sobbed. Arthur and a couple of other kids ran to the door. They looked out into the hall. Teachers were still screaming in various parts of the building. Down the hall, feathers ruffled in every direction, running like mad, was a giant chicken. The chicken waved its wings every time a classroom door was opened—and the teacher opening the door would scream or faint.

Arthur ran after Henrietta. By the time he got to the front door of the school, which was still swinging, Henrietta was out of sight. He ran out into the street, and looked in both directions, but there was no sign of her.

Everybody was sent home. School was closed until further notice. The teachers had a meeting, and demanded protection. They said their contracts did not require them to work in the presence of wild chickens.

Arthur came through the door at eleven-o-clock. "What are you doing home so early?" his mother asked.

"There was a chicken-scare," Arthur said, "we all got sent home until further notice."

VIII

The chicken-scare was not limited to Arthur's school. The whole town was chicken-panicky. The police department's switchboard received thousands of calls from frightened people. The mayor's office was full of citizens demanding protection from the giant chickens. Schools were closed. People were afraid to go shopping, to go to work, to step outside their doors. Special police chicken squads were sent to cruise the streets in cars. They had nets to capture the giant chickens. Helicopters buzzed over the rooftops, looking for chickens. Men stayed home from work to protect their families. Neighboring towns sent fire trucks, and teams of veterinarians to help in the chicken emergency.

Arthur was desperate to find Henrietta before some policeman threw a net over her. It wasn't easy to get out of the house. Momma and Poppa were convinced that it wasn't Henrietta, but some larger, wilder chickens that were causing all the trouble.

Arthur tried to be home for the six-o-clock news every night. He was trying to see if there was a pattern to Henrietta's movements from the television news reports. As far as he could tell, there was not. Henrietta turned up in different parts of Hoboken, sometimes blocks and blocks away from one another. She would be seen in four or five places in a single night.

THE GIANT CHICKEN WAS SEEN EMERGING FROM THE CLAM BROTHERS SEAFOOD RESTAURANT AT FOUR-FIFTY-SEVEN THIS MORNING. . . . the television newscaster would say. People had finally realized that there was only one chicken, not a whole flock. . . . THE RESTAURANT KITCHEN WAS A SHAMBLES, AND FORTY-SIX POUNDS OF FROZEN FRENCH-FRIED POTATOES WERE EATEN BY THE GIANT BIRD. HOBOKEN POLICE OFFICERS SMITH AND MOONEY GAVE CHASE IN THEIR SQUAD CAR, AND CORNERED THE CHICKEN ON COURT STREET, NEAR THIRD. THE CHICKEN THEN KICKED A HUGE DENT IN THE LEFT FRONT FENDER OF THE SQUAD CAR, WHICH INTERFERED WITH STEERING, AND RAN OFF INTO THE NIGHT. OFFICERS SMITH AND MOONEY WILL RECEIVE DECORATIONS FROM THE MAYOR AT A CEREMONY IN

HOBOKEN CITY HALL, TOMORROW AFTER-
NOON.

There were reports on the six o'clock news every
night. The giant chicken broke into restaurants and food
stores, overturned garbage cans, and beat up a number
of German shepherd dogs. Arthur worried that being
hunted was turning Henrietta mean.

The chicken-panic was turning into a deep depression.
People had chickens on their minds all the time. There
was an ugly situation outside a poultry market, which
nearly turned into a riot. Bus drivers refused to accept
assignments which routed their buses through Hoboken.
Schools were closed, and absenteeism at work was over
fifty per-cent. The mayor, who was planning to run for
re-election the next year, had received a great many nasty
letters and telephone calls. Half the police department
was on sick-leave, and the fire department had a new
policy of not responding to any chicken calls, saying
that chicken-control was the job of the police department. The chief of police said that his men were not
trained or equipped for chicken-control—it was the job
of the Hoboken dog-warden. The Hoboken dog-warden,
the most unpopular man in town, had vanished, and
nobody knew where he was. The state police had issued
a statement to the effect that chickens were a local problem, unless they interfered with traffic on state highways,
and the F.B.I. was not answering its telephone.

Day after day passed with no relief from the chicken
situation. Television stations and newspapers stopped

reporting chicken stories. Schools re-opened, and people began to go back to their jobs. Still, there were screams in the night. Brakes screeched, and people shouted when Henrietta appeared in the darkness. Nobody liked the situation, and the blame for not finding a solution was placed on the mayor and city council. It was the second week of December, and nothing had been proposed that seemed likely to do any good. The mayor was very unpopular. His advisors told him that the chicken stood a better chance of being elected than he did. The mayor took this very much to heart.

He called a special meeting of the city council. The members noticed that the mayor was smiling. He had not smiled since a few days after Thanksgiving. "Gentlemen," the mayor said, "I have here a letter from someone who can help us." He showed them a letter. It had a printed letterhead which read:

ANTHONY DE PALMA—CHICKEN HUNTER
Henfanger, Florida   Cable: SNATCH

The mayor held the letter over his head, so all the councilmen could read the letterhead. "Gentlemen, you may remember that in nineteen-fifty-seven, the city of Gatorade, Florida was plagued by a renegade rooster, known as Everglade Ike. This rooster was so destructive, that more than half the population of Gatorade fled their homes. In nineteen-sixty-two, there was an outbreak of chicken vandalism in Mooseport, Pennsylvania. A Pennsylvania State Forest Ranger was besieged in his cabin for seventy-two hours by a band of rogue chickens.

Also in nineteen sixty-two, an enraged hen occupied the movie theater in Swineford, New York, consumed fifty bushels of popcorn, slashed the seat cushions, and ran the movie, SPARTACUS, with Kirk Douglas, more than a hundred times until she was captured. In every one of these cases, the man who ultimately captured the renegade chickens was Mr. Anthony DePalma, of Henfanger, Florida. Mr. DePalma has captured the Himalayan Giant Capon, the only one in captivity; and he is the only man ever to have seen the rare Gaboon Pullet in its natural habitat. Mr. DePalma has written to me, and offered to help Hoboken with its chicken problem. I have taken the liberty of sending him a cable asking him to come at once. He will be here the day after tomorrow."

The city council broke into loud applause and cheering. The political opponents of the mayor stared at each other angrily—why hadn't they found out about Anthony DePalma? If he caught the chicken, the mayor would be re-elected for certain.

One of the mayor's supporters on the city council proposed that the city prepare a hero's welcome for Anthony DePalma. A hurried vote was taken, and the councilmen scurried off to outdo one another in preparing a welcome for the famous chicken-catcher.

Special editions of the newspapers came out, announcing that Anthony DePalma, world-famous chicken-catcher and adventurer was coming to rid Hoboken of its night-marauding chicken. Banners were strung across

Washington Street, and the fire department band was told to stand by. A reviewing stand was built overnight outside the city hall, and a parade was planned.

Arthur heard the news along with everyone else. He had given up hope of ever finding Henrietta—she had become too cagey to find—but he knew she was free and happy, and that gave him some comfort. The idea of Henrietta being caught by the famous chicken-catcher upset him. They would probably keep her in a cage. He wrote a postcard, and mailed it to Prof. Fritz Mazzocchi, c/o Cosima Mazzocchi, Mooseport, Pa. It said: "Famous chicken-catcher, Anthony DePalma, coming here to capture number seventy-three. Yours truly, Arthur Bobowicz."

IX

The mayor and the city council went to bed in a state of great excitement, the night before Anthony De-Palma was expected to arrive. Extra street sweepers had been put to work, there was a non-scheduled garbage collection, and all the lamp posts on Washington Street, had, in addition to Christmas decorations, papier-mache chickens attached to them with wires. Banners which read: HOBOKEN WELCOMES ANTHONY DE-PALMA were strung across Washington Street. The reviewing stand outside the city hall was hung with red-white-and-blue bunting, and cardboard chickens, covered with silver foil. Everything was ready for the big day.

Sometime after midnight, parked in the shadows outside the Hotel Victor, at the foot of River Street, was an old and battered red van. Lettered on the doors was the

name, A. DE PALMA, HENFANGER, FLA. Painted
on the back of the van was a chicken with a net over it.
I SNATCH FOR SCRATCH, it said underneath the
picture.

The patrolman on duty had reported the arrival of
Anthony DePalma's van to the sergeant-on-duty, in the
morning, the sergeant-on-duty reported it to the chief-of-
police, and the chief-of-police reported it to the mayor.
By eight-o-clock, the fire department band was lined up
outside the Hotel Victor, with the chief-of-police, the
fire chief, and three of the mayor's favorite city councilmen. They were a guard of honor, to escort Anthony
DePalma to the reviewing stand outside the city hall,
with the band playing, where the mayor would present
Anthony DePalma with a key to the city. Then a signal
would be given, and Anthony DePalma, the mayor, and
the city council would watch the parade. The leader of
the fire department band walked up and down, checking
to see that every man's buttons were shiny.

Nobody knew what Anthony DePalma looked like, so
there were several false starts, when ordinary guests came
out of the hotel. The mayor had told the band to play
something appropriate. They played *Turkey In The
Straw*. It was as close as they could come to something
about chickens. When Anthony DePalma finally did
come out, there was no doubt in anyone's mind that he
was the man to catch Hoboken's giant chicken. There
was something hard and steely in his gaze. He moved
with slow deliberate ease. This was a man who didn't

60

scare easily. He had lived with chickens. He could think like a chicken. There was more of the chicken about him than the man. Everybody was very impressed.

Anthony DePalma was wearing baggy green trousers, a flowered sport shirt, and a plaid jacket. On his head he had a white fisherman's hat with the name TONY embroidered in red on the brim. He was smoking a cigarette. He wore ankle-high basketball shoes. He was the very picture of a professional sportsman. The police chief, and the fire chief, and the councilmen shook hands with him. The band played *Turkey In The Straw*, and Anthony DePalma walked with the guard of honor to the city hall.

A messenger had run ahead with the news that Anthony DePalma was coming, and the mayor, and the rest of the city council were waiting on the reviewing stand. There was a small crowd, mostly early shoppers. The mayor made a short speech, and handed the key to the city of Hoboken to Anthony DePalma. A whistle was blown, and the Hoboken police, fire department, sanitation workers, and city employees began to pass in review.

"Let's go inside, and talk about money," Anthony DePalma said to the mayor, "I'm freezing my butt out here."

X

Anthony DePalma sat on the mayor's desk. He was picking his teeth with the mayor's letter-opener. "Sixty-thousand dollars, in advance," Anthony DePalma said. "Take it or leave it."

The mayor and the city council looked at one another nervously. "That's a very great sum of money," the mayor said.

"O.K. Live with your chicken. Goodbye." Anthony DePalma stood up, and started walking toward the door.

"Wait!" the mayor and city council shouted, "we'll pay!"

Anthony DePalma settled down to explaining his requirements for catching the giant chicken. "First of all, the chicken has to have a name," Anthony DePalma said.

"Excuse me," the mayor said, "I don't understand what the chicken's name has to do with catching it."

"It's for the newspapers," Anthony DePalma said, "It makes a better story. Didn't you read about Everglade Ike? It makes the chicken seem like more of a challenge. Like Moby Dick—not just some bum of a whale—Moby Dick! It's scarier. Let's call her Dirty Louise. Now, I think the best way to catch this chicken is in a trap. I can set a trap that no chicken can resist. Once I get my trap set up, nobody is to go near it. Wild chickens are very suspicious, and if they see or smell people they scoot. I'm going to set up my foolproof trap, and nobody is to go near it for five days. Then you'll collect your chicken."

"Please excuse me for asking, Mr. DePalma," the mayor said, "but how do we know this trap of yours is going to work?"

"O.K. That does it. You don't want to catch Dirty Louise—you don't have to catch Dirty Louise. I'm going." Anthony DePalma made for the door again. Three councilmen dragged him back, and sat him down in the mayor's chair. Everyone apologized to Anthony DePalma at once for seeming to doubt him. "Really I should go," he said, "There's a very nasty duck in Larchmont, N.Y., and the town council there is offering me one hundred thousand dollars and a new Rolls Royce. I *will* go. Chickens are too easy. I'm bored. I don't want the job."

The mayor and the city council begged Anthony DePalma to change his mind. Anthony DePalma kept

eyeing the door. They appealed to his mercy, his good-nature—nothing worked. Finally the mayor pointed out the window. Parked outside the city hall was the new semi-official mayoral limousine. It was painted powder-blue, and all the chromework had been gold-plated, there was an official Hoboken city seal in gold on either side, and it had a red flashing light, and a siren. "We'll throw that in!" the mayor shouted. He was almost crying; he had only taken one ride in the limousine, and he had never worked the siren.

"Well, since you're all such sincere men, I guess I could devote a few days to catching Dirty Louise for you."

"Just between us," Anthony DePalma said, "I have a secret weapon, that never fails with chickens. If you will keep it a secret, I'll show it to you when I get the trap set up." The mayor and the city council were very pleased that Anthony had decided to share this confidence with them, and all the men shook hands warmly, before they left the room.

XI

Anthony had chosen the Hoboken Little League field as the place to set up the chicken trap. Twenty-four hour police guards were set around the outside of the field, and instructions were published warning the citizens of Hoboken to stay away from the Little League field. Newspapers carried stories about Dirty Louise, and Anthony DePalma was interviewed on the television news.

The trap itself was concealed by a sort of canvas fence. It looked like a circus tent without a top. Anthony DePalma had unloaded bales of wire, lengths of wood, springs, rubber innertubes, cowbells, garbage can lids, coils of rope, and a lot of other materials. Now he was inside the topless tent, singing and hammering, while the policemen guarded the Little League field. When

the trap was finished, Anthony DePalma invited the mayor to come and look at the secret weapon. The mayor came and brought his favorite councilmen with him. Anthony met them at the entrance to the field.

"Gentlemen, I hope you will keep secret what you see here today. I rely on your absolute discretion." The mayor and the councilmen promised they would never speak a word about what Anthony DePalma was about to show them. They went into the topless tent.

"This, gentlemen, is Frankie. He is a judas-chicken. As you can see, Frankie is irresistible. He is more attractive than any chicken living." Anthony DePalma was gesturing to a chicken, about five feet tall. The chicken looked strangely like Anthony DePalma. It had a neat black moustache, black hair, with lots of hair oil, and it was smoking a cigarette. The feathers had a funny appearance, as though they were made of bits and pieces of styrofoam Dixie-cups. The chicken did not move. "What you have not noticed," Anthony DePalma went on, "is that Frankie is not a real chicken. He is a robot, or chickenoid. You may not believe this, but those are not real feathers. They are bits and pieces of styrofoam Dixie-cups. Frankie is powered by a twelve-volt car battery. He can sing, wink his eyes, blow smoke rings, and nod his head. No female chicken on earth can resist Frankie. When Dirty Louise sees Frankie, she will walk right into the trap. Just leave the trap, the Little League field, and the whole area, totally alone, for five days. At the end of that time, you can come and collect Dirty Louise."

The mayor and the councilmen were very impressed. Anthony DePalma threw a switch, and Frankie, the chickenoid began to nod his head, wink his eyes, blow smoke rings, and sing *Deep in the Heart of Texas.* The mayor and the councilmen filed out. They were sure that Anthony DePalma's chicken trap was the best investment the city of Hoboken had ever made. Anthony DePalma drove off in the powder-blue semi-official mayoral limousine. He had the red light flashing, and he was working the siren. He was never seen in Hoboken again.

Five days later, the combined police, fire and sanitation departments came to the chicken trap. They found one dachshund, two grey-and-black striped cats, a pigeon, and an old man named Meehan, who was singing *Deep in the Heart of Texas* with Frankie, the chickenoid. There was no Dirty Louise. During the five days in which the citizens of Hoboken had waited to see if Dirty Louise would turn up in the trap, she had hijacked a potato-chip truck, kicked over a fire-hydrant, and bent the flag-pole outside the senior high school. Nothing had changed. The mayor had spent sixty-thousand dollars of the town's money, and given away the semi-official limousine. Christmas was coming, and no one seemed to care.

XII

Arthur had received a post-card: MEET DOCTOR
HSU TING FENG AT THE RAILROAD STATION
AT 6:30 P.M. ON TUESDAY. It was not signed, but
it was postmarked MOOSEPORT, PA. Arthur was there
when the train pulled in. An old man got off. He looked
remarkably like Professor Mazzocchi, except that he had
a long moustache, and kept his hands inside the opposite
sleeves of his coat. "You are Arthur Bobowicz?" the old
man asked. "Kindly tell me everything about your rela-
tionship with number seventy-three."

On Wednesday morning, the mayor's secretary
brought a card to the mayor. It said:

Dr. Hsu Ting Feng
Poultry locator
(not a fake)

"You may as well send him in," the mayor said, "but I'm not going to pay him a penny."

"It will not be necessary for you to pay me a penny," Dr. Hsu Ting Feng said, when he had been shown into the mayor's office. "I am prepared to locate Dirty Louise, whose real name is Henrietta, also known as number seventy-three, purely as an exercise in philanthropy."

"I beg your pardon?" the mayor said.

"I mean to say, I'll catch the chicken, and not charge you anything," the old man said.

"We've already had one chicken expert, you know," the mayor said.

"Yes, I am acquainted with Mr. DePalma," Dr. Hsu said, "He was my pupil years ago. A young man not without talent, but slapdash, and huckle-muckle in his workmanship."

"What did you say?" the mayor asked. "He's a jerk," Dr. Hsu Ting Feng said.

"What exactly do you want from me?" the mayor asked.

"Only your cooperation," said the old man. "Please listen to my plan."

"Chickens are very sensitive birds," Dr. Hsu told the mayor, "It is very easy to hurt their feelings. When their feelings are hurt, they become unpleasant, anti-social. A perfectly sweet chicken can become a bitter destructive bird, if it feels that it is unwanted."

"Do you think that Dirty Louise . . ." the mayor began.

"Refer to her as Henrietta," Dr. Hsu interrupted, "it

72

will help you to think of her as a person, a misunderstood chicken, and a person."

"Excuse me; Henrietta," the mayor went on, "Do you think Henrietta is a chicken like that? Do you think she feels unwanted, and that's why she's kicking over fire-hydrants, and frightening the citizens?"

"I am sure of it," Dr. Hsu said. "I have found out that Henrietta was, for a short time, the personal pet of a young boy in this town. His name is Arthur Bobowicz. Young Arthur and Henrietta got to be great friends. Henrietta got into a tiny bit of trouble, and Arthur's parents insisted he take Henrietta back."

"Back? Back where?" the mayor asked, "Where did the bird . . ."

"Henrietta," Dr. Hsu interrupted.

"Where did Henrietta come from in the first place?"

"I haven't been able to find that out," Dr. Hsu said, "and if you want my help, you will have to promise not to look into that side of things at all."

"I agree, if you can stop these chicken outrages," the mayor said, "please continue with what you were saying."

"Arthur and Henrietta got to be great friends, and the boy's parents didn't want him to keep her. You know how these things happen in families. Henrietta missed Arthur, and set out to look for him. Every time people saw her, they screamed and ran away. They called the police, and the police chased her. She was hungry. She felt unloved. Think if it happened to you. You'd be angry too."

"This is perfectly reasonable," said the mayor, "but how will it help us to stop Henrietta's prowling at night?"

"I was coming to that," said Dr. Hsu. "First we have to get in touch with the Bobowicz family, and ask them if they are willing to give Henrietta another chance. If they agree, we will begin a campaign of publicity. We will encourage the citizens of Hoboken to have a friendly attitude toward chickens. We will ask them to wave and smile when they see Henrietta, instead of screaming, or calling the police, or throwing things at her. After a while, Henrietta may try to find Arthur again. If she does, she will be allowed to stay with them, like any normal two-hundred and sixty-six pound pet chicken. The town of Hoboken will issue her a chicken license, and everything will return to normal."

"It's worth a try," the mayor said.

The following day posters were printed. They showed a boy, looking very much like Arthur Bobowicz, with his arm around a big chicken. Special notices were printed in English, Spanish, Italian, Polish, and Hindi asking the people of Hoboken to wave and say hello, and smile, if they saw Henrietta. The Goodyear blimp was sent for, and it cruised back and forth over Hoboken, towing a large banner which read CHICKENS NEED YOUR LOVE. At night, the message was flashed in electric lights. The television stations cooperated. There were

special panel discussions on the late night talk-shows, in which psychologists and guidance experts told about chickens' need for love and approval. So that they wouldn't upset Henrietta, big white chickens were painted on all the police cars.

Arthur's father had been very honored when the mayor had come to see him in person, in the old, last year's semi-official mayoral limousine. He told the mayor that he'd be willing to give Henrietta another chance. The mayor told Mr. Bobowicz that he was a good citizen.

There was nothing to do but wait. All of Hoboken had received the word: *Be nice to the giant chicken.* The first couple of nights of the LOVE-HENRIETTA campaign passed without any sightings reported. On the third night, Hoboken police officers, Noonan and Feeney were driving in their squad-car. They had just turned the corner of Jackson and Willow, and were proceeding north on Jackson, when they saw something large and white in their headlights. It was Henrietta. She was standing in the middle of the street, facing the approaching squad car. It looked as though she wanted a fight. Noonan and Feeney remembered what had happened to the squad car belonging to Mooney and Smith. They stopped some distance from Henrietta, and got out of the car. Both police officers had been issued a large Idaho potato, and they were carrying them.

"Nice chicken," Officer Noonan said. "Nice Henrietta, want a potato?" Officer Feeney said. Henrietta cocked her head. She looked at the two policemen quizzically. The policemen took a step or two forward. Henrietta growled at them. They stopped, and put the large Idaho potatoes down on the street. Then Officers Noonan and Feeney got back into the squad car, backed it around the corner, and drove away. The last thing Henrietta saw was the big white chicken painted on the side of the squad car.

The following night Mr. and Mrs. Adolph Moscowitz were taking an evening stroll. Like most of the women in Hoboken, Mrs. Moscowitz had a bag of potato chips in her purse, in case of meeting Henrietta. Outside the park on Hudson Street, Henrietta confronted them. Mr. and Mrs. Moscowitz resisted the impulse to scream, run, or throw things at Henrietta. Instead, Mrs. Moscowitz held out the bag of potato chips, and said, "Nice chicken. Nice chicken." Henrietta stepped forward cautiously, took the bag of potato chips in her beak, and ran off into the night.

The following day, a group of children were having a game of fleegle in a schoolyard. They became aware that Henrietta was watching them from behind some garbage cans. They continued the game, but contrived to throw the fleegle closer and closer to Henrietta, until they were playing right in front of Henrietta's hiding place. While they played, they spoke softly to her, "Nice Henrietta. Nice chicken. Nobody's going to hurt you." Henrietta stayed during the entire game. On one occasion, someone threw the fleegle toward Henrietta. It landed at her feet. She pushed it toward the children with her beak. At the end of the game, the children went home as if nothing unusual had happened.

The next morning, people on their way to work noticed that Henrietta was sitting on the roof of the Hoboken Land and Improvement Building. Most of the people waved to her. "Good morning, Henrietta!" they shouted. Henrietta stayed on the roof, watching people come and go, for most of the morning. Then, suddenly, she was gone.

At noon, Henrietta walked through the swinging doors of the Clam Brothers Seafood Restaurant and Bar, made her way through the lunchtime crowd, and stopped at the free lunch counter. She ate some potato salad. "Hi, Henrietta! How ya' doing, Henrietta?" the patrons said. Somebody bought Henrietta a large root beer.

That afternoon, several people saw Henrietta in the deserted playground. She was playing on the slide.

People couldn't remember why they had been afraid of Henrietta. She seemed to be a very pleasant, well-behaved chicken. They liked her.

XIII

Arthur had just gone to bed, when Henrietta appeared on the fire escape outside his window. He opened the window, and let her in, hugged her, and scratched her head. Henrietta went to sleep on the rug next to Arthur's bed.

In the morning, Arthur's mother made some home-fried potatoes for Henrietta. His little brother and sister played with her, and fussed over her. Arthur's father telephoned the mayor, to say that Henrietta had come home.

It was just five days before Christmas, and the Hoboken police, fire, and sanitation department combined glee clubs had come to the city hall to serenade the mayor. Lots of people, especially children, had come into the city hall to hear the Christmas carols. The mayor came

out of his office with Henrietta and Arthur Bobowicz. The crowd cheered. The mayor waved for silence, "I am honored to bestow upon Henrietta, belonging to Arthur Bobowicz, of this city, the first official city of Hoboken Chicken License," the mayor said. He hung a ribbon around Henrietta's neck. Hanging from the ribbon was a bright metal disc. There were letters stamped on it. It said:

City of Hoboken
Incorporated 1855
Official Chicken License
No. 1

The crowd cheered and applauded, and the police, fire, and sanitation department combined glee clubs sang FOR SHE'S A JOLLY GOOD FELLOW. Everybody wanted to shake Arthur Bobowicz's hand, and pet Henrietta. Arthur's father was there, smoking a big cigar, the mayor had given him. He looked very proud of his son and his chicken.

XIV

On the day after Christmas, Arthur gave a show with Henrietta, at the playground. All the kids in the neighborhood were there. Henrietta had been a little rusty after all her weeks of running wild, but with a little practice, she was as good as ever on the swing, the slide, and some new tricks too. Henrietta had learned to jump fences all on her own, and Arthur was also able to teach her front somersaults. It was a good show. All the kids said they wished they could have a chicken like Henrietta.

After the chicken-show in the playground, Arthur and Henrietta went home for some more of Arthur's mother's Christmas potato-pie. Then, he and Henrietta went out to look for a secluded spot, where Henrietta could practice on Arthur's new Christmas roller-skates.